Eddie's Eclipse

Written by Becky Newsom & Pam Tucker

Illustrated by Pam Tucker

ISBN: 1548456217
ISBN-13: 978-1548456214

DEDICATION

To our ever curious, young scientists Camden, Morgan, Nolan and Sydney.
Keep exploring, experimenting and creating chaos.

One hot summer evening, there were so many stars above,
it looked like millions of diamonds dancing in the night. The
sliver of the crescent moon was the only other object to be
seen. That evening, a baby boy was born.

Under the brilliant sky, his parents named him Eddie, after world-famous astronomer, Edwin Hubble. An astronomer is a special kind of scientist who studies the planets, stars and space. In the early 1900's, Mr. Hubble helped discover that there were many galaxies beyond our own Milky Way Galaxy.

Edwin Hubble was so important in the science world, that the Hubble Space Telescope was named after him. Eddie's parents loved science and wanted to honor this special man by naming their son after him too.

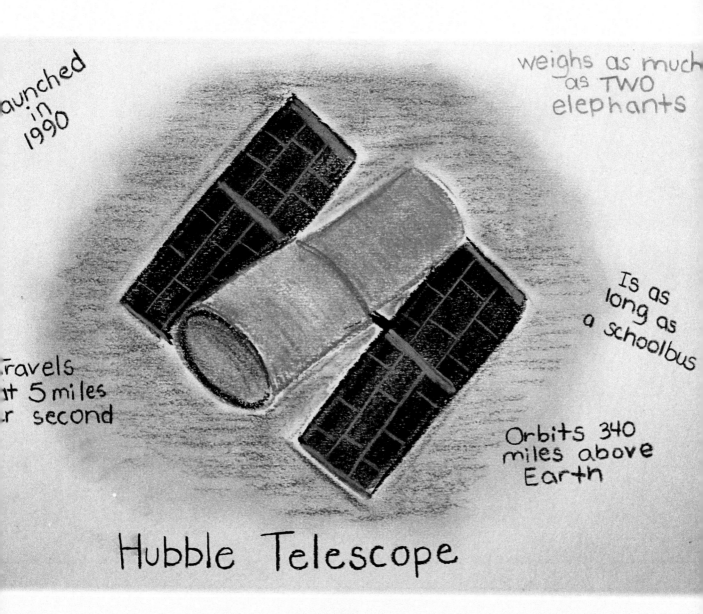

launched in 1990

weighs as much as TWO elephants

Is as long as a schoolbus

Travels at 5 miles per second

Orbits 340 miles above Earth

Hubble Telescope

As Eddie grew up, he became more and more fascinated by science. Many young boys loved sports or playing with cars and trains. Eddie loved playing with slime, insects and microscopes instead.

A natural curiosity inspired Eddie to wonder how things worked and why things happened. Once, he took apart his favorite bicycle and tried to build a robot with all of the pieces. It didn't work out so well, but he had a lot of fun trying.

Even when Eddie created messes and chaos, his mom and dad always encouraged his love for exploring and experimenting.

Science was Eddie's passion and the science center near his home was always his favorite place to visit. The energy wheel and the giant dinosaurs were among his favorite exhibits.

It seemed like he had been there a million times, yet each time he explored the science center, Eddie learned something new.

During his latest visit, Eddie learned about something very special that would be happening soon. The science center was preparing for the Great American Solar Eclipse on August 21, 2017.

AUGUST 21ST, 2017

When Eddie heard about this AMAZING news, he could hardly control his excitement. Like a true scientist, he wanted to learn all he could about this once-in-a-lifetime event.

The library was his first stop on the way home. Eddie knew that if he was going to become a "solar eclipse expert" he would have to begin his research right away.

He spent hours at the library reading books, exploring databases and searching through science magazines. By the time he was ready to leave, Eddie's head was so full of new knowledge he could hardly think.

On his way home from the library, Eddie's excitement turned to dread. As soon as he walked through the door, his mom noticed that something wasn't right.

"What's wrong, Eddie?" she asked. "Why do you look so sad?"

Eddie explained that he would be in school on the day of the solar eclipse. He was devastated to think that he would miss the spectacular event.

Eddie's mom reassured him that his school would celebrate this event and do something special for all of the students. After all, school was where kids go to learn and this solar eclipse was going to be an incredible learning experience.

The following week, Eddie woke up and was bouncing with excitement! Not only was a new school year about to begin, but the eclipse was only a few days away. Eddie was hopeful that his mom was right and his school would be doing something extraordinary to celebrate the eclipse.

As Eddie walked into class for the first time, he met his new teacher, Mrs. Beaker. During that first day, he and his classmates spent what seemed like forever getting to know one another. They found their new seats and discussed the class rules. Mrs. Beaker told them about all of the exciting things they would be learning this year.

Eddie loved getting to know his new teacher and classmates, but something was missing.

Eddie wondered if his mom had been wrong. Maybe his school wasn't going to do anything special for the upcoming solar eclipse. And then it finally happened. This was the moment Eddie had been waiting for.

"In just a few short days, a very special event will take place," Mrs. Beaker explained.

She revealed how his school had spent months planning for the upcoming solar eclipse and told the students that they would all get the opportunity to witness something extraordinary.

The class listened intently as Mrs. Beaker began her science lesson. She told them that the Moon constantly orbits, or travels, around the Earth. Sometimes their paths cross and the Moon moves directly between the Sun and Earth. When that happens, the Moon blocks out some of the Sun's rays and casts a shadow on the Earth. This phenomenon is known as a solar eclipse.

Mrs. Beaker explained that on August 21st, all of North America will be able to observe a partial solar eclipse. The Sun, Moon and Earth will be almost exactly aligned in space, allowing the Moon to block out part of the Sun's light.

"During a partial eclipse, the Sun looks like a bite has been taken out of it," Mrs. Beaker said.

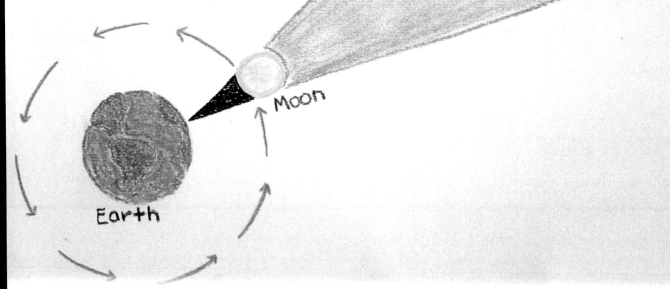

United States

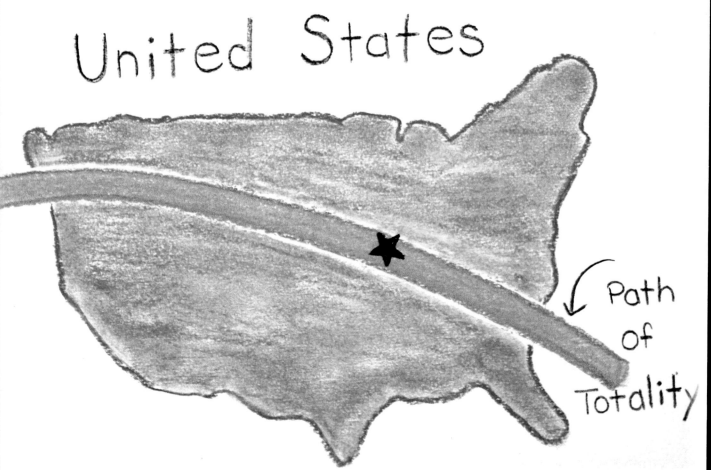

Path of Totality

Eddie thought that seeing a partial solar eclipse sounded pretty AMAZING. Then, Mrs. Beaker told the class something even more unbelievable.

This eclipse was extra-special for Eddie and his classmates because his school was located in an area known as the "Path of Totality". Eddie and his friends would get to witness a *TOTAL SOLAR ECLIPSE*. For just a few moments, the Sun, Moon and Earth will be perfectly aligned, allowing the Moon to block out all of the Sun's rays . During that time, the sky will go dark. Sometimes, stars will appear and the temperature outside may even drop. It is like nighttime in the middle of the day.

Eddie learned that the "Path of Totality" for the upcoming eclipse will stretch from coast to coast allowing kids from 14 different states to witness the breathtaking total solar eclipse.

Mrs. Beaker told Eddie and his classmates that people would be coming to his town from all around the world to view the Great American Solar Eclipse.

MONTANA
KANSAS
IOWA
ILLINOIS
North Carolina
OREGON
MISSOURI
Idaho
GEORGIA
NEBRASKA
Wyoming
TENNESSEE
SOUTH CAROLINA
KENTUCKY

Mrs. Beaker explained that a solar eclipse occurs somewhere on Earth about once every 18 months. However, you have to be in the right place at the right time to see one.

During each eclipse, the path of totality is only visible to a small part of Earth and many times is located over the ocean where no one is around to see it.

That means, only a few lucky people get to witness each spectacular solar eclipse.

According to Mrs. Beaker, a total solar eclipse hasn't been seen in Eddie's town since 1442. That was a long time ago... even before Christopher Columbus explored the Americas!

Mrs. Beaker continued to tell her class that although they want to see the eclipse, it is very dangerous to look directly at the Sun. Eddie began to worry until he learned that each student would get his or her own pair of solar eclipse glasses to wear on the big day.

These glasses have special lenses that block out the Sun's harmful rays and help protect their eyes.

Eddie imagined looking like a superhero while wearing his awesome glasses.

The night before the eclipse, Eddie tossed and turned and just could not fall asleep. He was so excited for everything that was about to happen. He watched the Moon out the window and hoped for a clear day tomorrow.

As Eddie finally drifted off to sleep, he had the biggest smile on his face. He knew that tomorrow was going to be a day he would remember for the rest of his life.

Eclipse day had finally arrived! Eddie brought his mom and dad to school with him so they could witness this amazing experience together. His parents would also help other students understand the day's events and help them remember how to stay safe during the eclipse.

The entire school gathered outside to make sure no one missed this once-in-a-lifetime event. Music played and friends chatted with one another as anticipation filled the air. Everyone wore their special glasses while they eagerly waited for the eclipse to become visible.

Eddie looked over at his school's countdown clock and saw that the eclipse was only moments away. He could hardly wait!

Mr. Petrie, the school Principal, made announcements to ensure that students kept their eyes safe.

As the Moon started passing in front of the Sun, a partial eclipse was visible. During that time, the Sun was still much too bright to look at directly. Mr. Petrie reminded the students that they needed to keep their glasses on to protect their eyes.

Finally, it was time for the total solar eclipse! When the Moon was completely in front of the Sun, Mr. Petrie announced that everyone could take off their glasses. It was only dark for just over a minute, but it was one of the best minutes of Eddie's life. For a very short time, it got dark outside, just like Mrs. Beaker said it would. Sometimes Eddie gets scared of the dark, but this was different...

It was science, and it was *AMAZING!!!*

When the sky brightened again, Eddie and his friends cheered and celebrated being a part of such a special day. Seeing the sky go dark in the middle of the day made Eddie love science even more than he already did.

On the way home from school that day, Eddie told his parents he would never forget the Great American Solar Eclipse. He dreamed about becoming a famous scientist one day. Eddie couldn't wait for his next scientific adventure!

Author's Note:

The concept of <u>Eddie's Eclipse</u> developed after learning of the behind the scenes work that was occurring within our school district to prepare thousands of students for the 2017 Great American Solar Eclipse. It was difficult to find child friendly resources to help educate students about this experience, so we decided to create our own.

Working in a school library gives us the opportunity to see how children's literature can engage students and aid in the understanding of sometimes difficult concepts. It is our hope that Eddie's story can help our youngest learners feel more at ease while experiencing the solar eclipse.

We named our main character Eddie as a tribute to Edwin Hubble, a famous astronomer who was born in Missouri. We take pride in this connection to the state we call home.

Additionally, we hope that Eddie's passion for all things science will inspire students to explore, experiment and create a little bit of chaos while learning something new.